A Heartwarming Inspirational Romance...

Family Ever After
by Linda Goodnight

With her bad-girl days behind her, new Christian Ashley Harcourt wanted to build a good life for her baby boy. Yet a reunion with a childhood flame brought old doubts to the fore—could a girl with a scarlet past ever win a good man?

Also enjoy a sneak preview of...

A Soldier's Heart
by Marta Perry
A Love Inspired® novel
On sale May 2007

After wounded army officer Luke Marino was sent home, he refused physical therapy. But Mary Kate Flanagan Donnelly needed Luke's case to prove herself as a capable therapist. If only it wasn't so hard to keep matters strictly business...

Dangerous Game
by Lyn Cote
A Love Inspired® Suspense novel
On sale May 2007

Returning home after spending time in prison, Grey Lawson was horrified to discover a new series of accidents that eerily mirrored events from his past. Deputy Trish Franklin had to tread carefully as she got involved with Grey, and he would have to pray she wouldn't suffer for his sins.

Look for valuable coupons inside!

STEEPLE HILL BOOKS

Steeple Hill®

Copyright © 2007 by Harlequin Books S.A.

ISBN-13: 978-0-373-15062-5
ISBN-10:   0-373-15062-8

The content of the excerpts in this book may have been edited from
their original format. The publisher acknowledges the copyright holders
of the excerpts from the individual works as follows:

Special thanks and acknowledgment are given to Linda Goodnight
for FAMILY EVER AFTER.

FAMILY EVER AFTER
Copyright © 2007 by Harlequin Books S.A.

Excerpt from A SOLDIER'S HEART
Copyright © 2007 by Martha P. Johnson

Excerpt from DANGEROUS GAME
Copyright © 2007 by Lyn Cote

www.SteepleHill.com

Printed in U.S.A.

CONTENTS

FAMILY EVER AFTER
Linda Goodnight

Steeple
Hill®

Published by Steeple Hill Books™

Chapter One

Ashley Harcourt finally had a handle on her life.

Maybe.

She hitched her baby boy higher on one hip and opened the wooden back gate leading through the colorful gardens between the cottages and the blacksmith shop. The metal clang of the smithy's hammer echoed through the summer morning.

A tiny thrill raced up Ashley's arms as it did every day since beginning her internship at the Colonial Williamsburg Department of Research and Design. She loved everything about the historic town, almost as much as she loved creating the clothes worn by the shopkeepers and tradesmen traversing the streets.

Best of all, here in Williamsburg she was just another intern, not a notorious Harcourt from Chestnut Grove.

Though the worst had died down, the unpleasant publicity hounding her family's connection to the embattled Tiny Blessings Adoption Agency provided enough reason for Ashley to love the idea of a summer away. Chestnut Grove was only a few miles down the road, so she could be away from the scandal—both her family's and that of her own making—yet remain close enough to see her family anytime she chose.

Yes, here in Williamsburg, she could enjoy America's past and hide from her own.

The smithy's hammering ceased.

"Ashley?" a male voice called from somewhere behind her.

Ashley stopped and whipped around, her long skirt circling her legs with fresh air. She'd only been here a week. Who could possibly be calling her name?

A lean, muscular figure exited the open door of the blacksmith shop and came toward her, dusty black boots crunching softly on the glittering oyster shell path. Dressed in a leather apron over knee breeches and a loose, muslin shirt opened at the throat, he looked like a blast from the past.

The thought froze in her head as recognition dawned. He *was* a blast from the past. The near past. Hers.

"Christopher?" she squeaked.

The man she'd turned her back on when she'd been young and stupid was here, in Williamsburg.

"It's me," he said, the familiar, crooked smile saying he was pleased to see her.

So much for hiding from the past.

"I saw you from the window," he continued, motioning toward the blacksmith shop behind him.

"Anyway, I thought it was you. What are you doing here in Williamsburg?"

His green-as-spring gaze took in her long, colonial-style dress. From his behavior, it appeared he bore her no ill will. She just didn't get that. Surely even Christians held grudges.

Well, what did it matter one way or the other what he thought of her? A guy like Chris would have found a great wife by now who was as good as he was. No doubt, he barely remembered his short-lived relationship with Ashley Harcourt. He didn't know it, but God had been looking out for him back then.

She shifted the baby a little higher on one hip and said, "I'm interning in the fashion department."

With a smile, Chris held his arms out to the side. "So you're the one making the interpreters' duds?"

"One of several. I'm still learning." And until this moment, she'd thought the internship was the answer to her prayers.

Guess not.

"That's great," he said. Laugh lines, always present around his mouth and eyes, deepened.

"So what are you doing here? I heard you became a minister."

"I did. A little church in modern Williamsburg not far from William and Mary, but you know how I always liked history. This is the best of both worlds. I can work on my master's thesis in historical trades, play with the forge and hammer and still take care of my church."

History was one of the things they'd had in common

back at Tarkington, the elite private school they'd both attended—she because her parents were filthy rich and he because he was smart enough to get a scholarship. She'd always envied him that brilliance. More than that, she'd envied his steadfast awareness of who he was and what he wanted out of life. Nothing ever shook Chris Sullivan. Faith and goodness emanated from him now as it did then.

"That's great." She noticed he didn't say one word about taking care of a family. Could someone like Chris still be single?

A tiny flame of something akin to hope flickered in her chest, but she immediately doused it.

Christopher was a nice guy. Good. Holy, even. And she was—well, she wasn't holy, that was for certain.

"So how have you been?" he asked.

"Busy." That was an understatement, considering the mess she'd made of her life. "You?"

"Yep. Crazy busy, but it's all good." She wished she could say the same. "What time is your lunch? We can go to Chownings for root beer and barbecue and catch up."

Catch up? As nice as that sounded, she didn't think so, given he was a minister and she an unwed mother with a guilt complex bigger than a colonial hoop skirt. God may have forgiven her, but she was still working on forgiving herself.

"I don't know, Chris. Sometimes the past is better left alone."

If he knew the depth of her sin, a sin far greater than having a child out of wedlock, he wouldn't even speak to her.

His green eyes turned serious. "Friends don't stop being friends because of a disagreement."

"You haven't changed at all, have you?"

He laughed. "Some. I hope for the better. So what do you say? Lunch later?"

While she struggled for a kind but firm way out of a reunion lunch, Chris turned his attention to the baby. "And who's this little guy?"

As usual, she'd waited too long to do the right thing. Story of her life.

Embarrassed heat rushed up the neck of her high lace collar, but she fought it off. She was ashamed of herself, but never of her baby.

"This is Gabriel," she said with quiet pride. "My son."

Something flickered in Chris's expression as he glanced from the baby to her. But it wasn't the censure she'd expected.

"So you married the guy," he said softly.

Heart thudding, she hitched her chin. "No. Actually, I didn't. He had other plans."

Denying any responsibility, Gabriel's father had headed for Europe the day after discovering her pregnancy. According to his family, Ashley was a climber trying to lay claim to the family's wealth and position. Had her own family not been wealthy, she could have understood their point. As it was, Roman's behavior only proved how wrong she'd been to trust him in the first place.

All the girls had wanted the new guy. He'd been exciting and wild, everything Chris wasn't. She'd been flattered when the sophisticated heir to one of D.C.'s most prominent families had cast his wandering eye and seductive smile in her direction. But no one had ever told her about men like Roman Fields.

To Chris's credit, he didn't press for the ugly details, though he had to be curious. Instead, he took Gabriel's reaching fingers and gave them a gentle shake. "Nice to meet you, little man."

Ashley's heart squeezed as her baby displayed four front teeth in a wide grin. There was something undeniably beautiful about a child's tiny hand wrapped around a man's long fingers. Especially this man's.

The thought jerked her to her senses. She could not, would not, let herself think such things.

Abruptly she said, "I have to go now."

As she deftly pried Gabriel's fingers loose, her skin brushed Chris's hand. The flutter in her belly was a warning she couldn't deny. "Can't be late to work. Sorry."

And she was. Sorry for all that she'd ruined. Sorry for the wrong she'd done. Sorry she'd lost all hope in the relationship department.

Chris took one step back, his arms falling to his side. "Sure. Okay."

She could hear the disappointment and hated herself for putting it there. But common sense screamed for her to escape before she did something really stupid, like ask if he was married.

If Ashley had hit him in the face with a mud brick, he couldn't have been more surprised. Or angry.

Though heat billowed from the fire, and sweat ran down his face, Chris didn't take a break from the forge.

Ashley Harcourt, the girl he couldn't forget—make that the *woman* he couldn't forget—was back in his life. They'd lost touch when he'd graduated, considering she was with Roman, while he was the voice crying in the wilderness, scared of what a cad like Roman would do to a gentle, insecure girl like Ashley. Might as well admit the truth. He'd been jealous, too.

He figured the Lord would understand if he wanted to punch the blue blood right out of Roman's nose.

Instead, he slammed the hammer down on the anvil with grim satisfaction.

She'd changed, matured. There was a sad wisdom in her brown eyes that hadn't been there in the old days. But she was still Ashley, the only woman he'd ever entertained any thoughts of marrying. From the first time he'd seen her in some funky-looking vintage hat he'd been in love with her, though she hadn't known it. He'd prayed a lot about her, especially after Roman came into the picture, and finally decided he had let his own will get in the way of God's. Sometimes it was hard to tell the two apart.

But now she was back.

The idea gave him pause. He stopped, hands on hips, and stared out the window in the direction she'd gone. She was here, at least for the summer. So was he.

That had to mean something.

Chapter Two

"Ow!" Ashley stuck her index finger into her mouth and sucked hard.

Milly, her boss, looked up from stitching a lace-edged cap. "Did you stick yourself with a needle again? What's wrong today, Ashley? I've never seen you so fumble-fingered." Then with a sly smile, the middle-aged woman added, "Wouldn't be that handsome smithy I saw you talking to, would it?"

Ashley's nerve endings jittered. She'd thought of little else all morning. It seemed as if every time she started making progress in her life, something came along to knock her backward.

No, that wasn't fair, nor was it correct. Chris Sullivan had been a good friend. He'd never done one thing to cause her pain. She'd caused her own problems. Didn't the Bible say she had to reap whatever she'd sown? And she had sown some very bad seed.

"Chris is an old friend," she said simply.

"That's good." Milly hitched a square chin toward the door just as the bell jangled overhead. "Because here he comes."

This time Ashley's stomach jumped into her throat. Chris had discarded the tradesman's apron but still wore seventeenth-century garb, as was required of all who worked in the town. His dark brown hair was slicked back and caught at the nape in a very short ponytail. She wondered what his congregation thought of that.

"It's lunchtime," he announced without preliminaries. "Right, Milly?"

The designer glanced at the watch pinned to her gingham bodice. "That it is, young man."

"Then you won't mind if I escort Miss Harcourt to Chownings. We have some catching up to do."

Milly eyed him over the rim of her skinny little bifocals. "Only if you promise to bring her back by one. Patrick Henry expects his new waistcoat today."

Chris chuckled. "Far be it from me to upset the fiery Mr. Henry. I'll have her back in time." He aimed a challenging grin at Ashley. "Grab whatever you need, and I'll get the little guy."

While Ashley grappled for bearings, he went straight to the playpen. Gabriel held up chubby arms and babbled happily as Chris scooped him up.

"Chris, I can't." She didn't need the grief or the reminders of what an idiot she'd been. Still was.

"Can't what? Eat?" By now Gabriel had latched on to Chris's ear. "Is this a medical problem I should know about? Everyone eats." He gave Gabriel a little bounce. "Isn't that right, champ?"

When Gabriel laughed, Ashley cracked a smile. "There's nothing wrong with my appetite."

"That's a relief. Sickly women scare me." Chris scooped an old-fashioned diaper bag onto his opposite arm and started toward the door with her baby. When she didn't move, he said, "Are you coming or is it just me and the little guy for lunch?"

The man had certainly changed from a docile, studious youth to a strong, forceful man. And the difference was rather thrilling.

"You'd kidnap my son?"

A dimple flashed in his right cheek. "Want to find out?"

"I might stand right here and see if you would do it."

He opened the door. Gabriel looked at her, puzzled for a moment, and then he waved bye-bye. Christopher burst out laughing. "I think he likes me."

So did she. That was the trouble.

Ashley studied his teasing expression for two beats before making up her mind. Chris was a friend. They were far enough away from Chestnut Grove to keep him from discovering her shameful secret, and right now she could use a good friend.

"All right," she sniffed, fighting the urge to laugh, too. "Anything to protect my son."

Behind her Milly snorted. Knowing her boss's propensity for romance novels and soap operas, Ashley let that slide right by. She needed friends, not a matchmaker. Later, she'd make it clear that there was nothing but friendship going on between her and Chris.

As they stepped out on the boardwalk, Christopher offered his elbow.

Ashley shook her head. "You have an old-fashioned diaper bag on there. I think that's probably enough."

Instantly, he shifted both baby and bag to one arm. "What's your excuse now, Miss Harcourt?"

She batted her eyelashes at him playfully. "And they say chivalry is dead."

His answer was a cocky grin.

She slid one hand into the crook of his elbow, the blacksmith's muscles strong beneath her fingertips. As they strolled along Duke of Gloucester Street, Chris kept up a joking commentary on the peculiarities of the various shopkeepers.

Christopher had always known how to make her laugh, had always been there to listen. For the first time in a long while, she felt relaxed and carefree again. A summer in the company of an old friend, far from the gossip of Chestnut Grove, might be a good thing after all. Catching up didn't have to include everything.

When they reached Chownings, tourists crowded the centuries-old eating establishment. In costume, she and Chris were obliged to act the part wherever they went. Chris was far better at it than she, doing so with grace, humor and amazing historical accuracy.

"You're good at this," she said when they were finally alone.

"Thanks. Do you like my ponytail?" He patted it. "It's new this summer."

"Charming. But it's the buckled shoes that really grabbed me."

Humor sparkled in his green eyes. "That's what all the women say. Wait until I don my tricornered hat. Turns me into a regular chick magnet."

They both laughed, but Ashley realized Chris *was* a chick magnet. He hadn't been in school, but that was only because of the snob mentality, which deemed him unworthy because he didn't come from a prominent family. Even then she'd recognized the lie in that. Chris had been worth more than all the money in that school. She just wished she'd realized it sooner.

The waitress came and they ordered sandwiches. When she left, Chris laced his fingers together on the table top. "All right now. Talk time. Where have you been? What have you been doing?"

She glanced at Gabriel in his highchair. "Well, I had a baby. Obviously." She gave a nervous laugh, expecting to be judged somehow less because of that.

"He's a happy baby. You must be a great mom."

Considering how bad a mother she'd once been, his compliment buoyed her. "Thanks. I'm trying."

"Raising a baby alone can't be easy."

"It isn't, but my parents help out some." She handed the baby a toy to keep him occupied. "So tell me about you? I thought you'd be a missionary in India by now."

"Those were my plans. The Lord had others. My

mom was diagnosed with lupus, so I needed to stay close to home."

"I'm sorry. I hope she's doing okay." Chris was all about family.

"Mom's tough. She's doing pretty well."

"What about your brothers? I thought they lived in Williamsburg, too."

"Mark does, but Sean's in the military. Mark has four kids, including a set of triplets. I figured he had his hands full."

She widened her eyes in pretend horror. "No kidding. One is a handful for me most of the time. Are you sorry you didn't make it to the mission fields?"

"Not even a little. The Lord showed me something pretty cool. There are mission fields everywhere, even here in Williamsburg. And He's such a good God. As soon as I made the decision to stay home, a new church plant opened up and asked me to take over the pastorate. It's small but growing so I'm bivocational for now. And even that's a good thing, a gift, because I can work here doing something else I love."

"So everything worked out perfectly for you."

He gave her a quizzical look. "Not everything. No luck yet finding the perfect woman. But I have a feeling God's not finished in that department."

Ashley let the sentence soak into her consciousness. For his sake, she hoped he didn't mean what she thought he meant, but just in case, she didn't ask.

Instead she said, "I'm a Christian now, too."

Saying the words still felt odd, but odd in a good way.

"I knew there was something different about you. Besides being a new mom."

"Is it a good difference or a bad difference?"

"Definitely good. You're more confident. More peaceful. Grown up, I guess."

If only he knew how scared she was all the time.

"When I was pregnant with Gabriel, I remembered what you'd told me about Jesus, about how He loves us even though we've messed up. Then I had some problems after Gabriel was born." Some of which she prayed he'd never heard about.

Christopher's eyes flared alarm. "Are you okay?"

"Oh, sure. I'm fine now." Physically, anyway. "But the crisis opened my eyes and I gave my life over to Him. I figured He could run it a lot better than I had."

"This is awesome, Ash. The best news ever."

Though she'd expected nothing less from Chris, she felt a little self-conscious. She might be a Christian, but she was far from perfect like Chris. "It's all still new, but I know I made the right choice."

"Yeah. Absolutely." He leaned forward as though he wanted to touch her but instead kept his elbows on the rough-hewn wooden table. The deep spirituality that had marked him as a target for both ridicule and respect at Tarkington flowed from him. He had always had a passion for God that she was only just now beginning to understand.

"You don't know how happy that makes me," he said. "And all that time whenever I talked about Jesus, you acted bored."

"Not bored, really. Uncomfortable and puzzled. I just didn't get it. But I was listening, too. You had something none of the rest of us had. A sense of purpose, a sense of who you were and what you wanted out of life."

"Oh, I had my doubts at times, especially at Tarkington."

"You?"

"Sure. It's not easy being the odd man out."

"I suppose not." In truth, she'd never considered how difficult it must have been for him. He'd never complained, but he'd also never had the money for the kinds of clothes and car and entertainment the rest of them enjoyed.

She'd had all that but still lacked the one thing he did have: happiness.

"So what are your big plans for the future?"

She hitched one shoulder. "To raise my son and hopefully to work my way into the head designer's job here someday. I'm entering the Independence Day contest with some of my best work. If I can win that, I'll automatically be invited to stay on as an apprentice."

The Independence Day Committee was holding a design contest this year in conjunction with the usual celebrations. Quilts, clothing, hats and any number of other stitched goods could be submitted by contestants around the globe. The prize winner could choose between a cash prize or an apprenticeship with the museum. Ashley wanted the coveted apprenticeship badly.

"You always did a have a sense of style." Chris tilted back in his chair, fingers absently rubbing the condensation from his root beer bottle. "I remember some of the outfits you put together. The floppy old hats and scarves and crazy color combinations you wore. A total individualist."

She'd been dying for attention while trying to hide the scared, confused Ashley behind her crazy costumes. She understood that now.

"When your sister is a beautiful model that everyone goes gaga over, you have to do something to stand out."

"You're every bit as beautiful as Samantha."

"I wasn't fishing for a compliment."

"Take it anyway. You always did sell yourself short."

"And you were the nicest guy on campus."

"Well, you know what they say about nice guys," he joked. "Last place."

She laughed. "Not true. Look at you."

A funny expression crossed his face, but before he could say more the waitress brought their food. Gabriel slapped the top of his highchair and made excited baby noises.

"Don't you ever feed this kid?" Chris softened the question with a grin.

"Trust me, he eats all the time. He loves food." As was evidenced by his chubby cheeks and thrashing legs.

"Even those?" Chris pretend shuddered as he pointed at a bowl of English peas. "Poor kid. Mind if I give him a French fry?"

"You'll be his best friend forever if you do."

"Can't beat a deal like that." He dipped the potato in ketchup and offered it to the wiggling child. "What about us, Ashley? Are we still friends?"

"I hope so." Friends, she could handle.

"Cool. Very cool. Mind if I say grace?"

"I'd be disappointed if you didn't." She folded her hands on the tabletop and closed her eyes.

After the quiet prayer, Chris winked at her. Then he popped a French fry into his mouth while handing another to Gabriel.

Some of the tension left Ashley's shoulders. If Christopher only had friendship in mind, he was safe…and so was her secret. They'd both be just fine for a summer.

Chapter Three

Christopher didn't know how much longer he could keep up the charade. After two weeks of finding excuses to see her, he was going a little crazy. But Ashley still held part of herself aloof, as though she was afraid of letting him get too close. Like a butterfly in one of Williamsburg's glorious gardens, she flitted just out of his reach.

She liked him. He was certain of that, but frankly, friendship wasn't enough. Smiling ruefully, he shook his head. *Friends*. What had he been thinking when he'd said such a goofball thing? He had lots of friends. He wanted a wife. He wanted Ashley. He wanted to be her white knight whether she needed one or not, the man she looked to, the man she needed in her life.

And this time he refused to be the odd man out, the kid who didn't fit. Here they were on equal footing.

He clicked the lock on the blacksmith shop and crossed the short distance to Ashley's cozy cottage. Last night, he'd weaseled an invitation to her place for spaghetti. Tonight it was lasagna. She was a horrible cook, but he would have eaten dirt and asked for seconds to see her smile.

He'd also promised his unbiased opinion on the historical gown she was hand-stitching for the July Fourth contest. Never mind that he was completely ignorant on the matter—he'd use any excuse to spend time with Ashley and little Gabriel.

Behind the heavy drapes of her living quarters, a light glowed. He lifted his knuckles to knock but before he could, Ashley yanked the door open.

"Get in here, quick." She plucked his shirt sleeve and tugged him inside.

He cast a furtive look behind him. "Don't tell me. The British are coming—again."

"No, silly, I want to show you something." She pointed to Gabriel, who stood hanging on to the couch, fat knees bobbing up and down in a baby dance. In a very short period of time, the little boy's constant smile and sweet nature had easily won him over, and it hadn't taken much. He was a sucker for kids.

Ashley motioned him toward the couch where she went down on her haunches in front of the baby and held out both arms. "Come to Mama, sugar pie."

Gabriel's bouncing stopped while he considered the request, but he didn't turn loose of the couch. Ashley tried again. "Come on, baby. Show Chris what a big boy you are. Walk to Mommy."

Still the baby didn't budge. The situation would have been funny if Ashley hadn't looked so disappointed.

"He took some steps not five minutes ago, and now he won't do it."

Chris squatted down and held out his arms. "Come on, champ. Show off for your Mama."

To his surprise, Gabe's eyes lit up and he stretched one hand in Chris's direction, hanging on to the couch with the other. In the next instant, he let go completely and toddled two steps into Chris's waiting arms.

"He did it, he did it," Ashley squealed. Chris knew exactly how she felt. Clasping Gabriel to his chest and laughing, he pivoted toward the excited mommy. With a whoop, she threw her arms around both the baby and him. Reflexively, he pulled her close.

The next thing he knew he was drowning in eyes as soft as brown velvet.

Was it his nearness that set her pulse tick-ticking against her collarbone? Or the thrill of seeing her baby walk?

Just in case it was both, he murmured, "Ash."

The corners of her lips tilted upward. She didn't move away, just held his gaze with hers.

And in that sweet, celebratory moment, Chris knew that this was meant to be his family. He, Ashley and Gabriel.

But before it could happen, he needed a small miracle. He needed Ashley to love him, too.

Ashley felt the rumble of Christopher's merry laughter give way to the steady thud-thud of his heartbeat. This close the gentle scent of shower soap and the strength of arms that wielded a smithy's hammer were a powerful combination, and a reminder that Chris might be a friend, but he was also a man.

She started to pull away, but Chris held fast.

"Ash," he said again, eyes searching hers, sculpted smile questioning.

He wanted to kiss her.

Not good. Not good at all.

Especially since she struggled with the longing to place her palm against his strong, square jaw and let him. But she liked him too much to go there. That was the trouble. She liked him way too much to ruin his life with the scandal that surrounded her.

Gently, so as not to hurt his feelings more, she transferred her arms from Chris to her son, putting the focus on Gabriel. Chris got the message and tilted back on his heels, still watching her.

While she fiddled with Gabriel's downy blond curls, Chris spoke quietly. "I have a confession to make."

Her gaze flicked up to his and back down to her son.

"Sounds serious."

"Remember a few weeks ago when I said I wanted us to be friends?"

Her fingers stilled. "Yes."

"That wasn't exactly true."

Ashley's heart skipped a beat. Either Chris had judged her and found her wanting, or worse, he hadn't. Either way, she was in trouble. She opted for what she deserved—judgment.

"It's okay. I understand."

"I don't think you do." Chris's voice remained soft,

the tone mesmerizing. The muscles in Ashley's shoulders, already stiff from hours over a needle and thread, bunched to a spasm.

Gabriel wiggled loose and crawled onto Chris's knee. As if he hardly noticed his actions, Chris bounced the baby up and down. Ashley cast around for something to say but her brain, like a drained battery, no longer functioned.

"Friendship is a good start, Ash," Chris said. "And I want that for us. But I want more."

The skittering pulse stopped and restarted.

"I don't understand." Or maybe she did. And the idea scared her out of her mind. Regardless of her feelings or of his, what he wanted was impossible….

"Here's the deal." Strong, calloused fingers found hers and squeezed. "I let you get away once before. I'd be a fool to let it happen again."

Fighting off a futile surge of hope, Ashley shook her head. Christopher the Christian, the nice guy turned minister, hadn't a clue what he was talking about. She was no prize. She wasn't the same innocent girl he'd known at Tarkington. As much as she liked him, she couldn't let him do this to himself.

She tried to tease away the seriousness. "Oh, no you don't, Christopher Sullivan. No fair changing the rules midgame."

"I'm serious, Ashley."

"Get real. You have a ton of women sending messages your way every day. I've seen them in the blacksmith shop, on the streets. You don't need me."

He drew in a ragged breath and blew it out. The puff of air stirred Gabe's curls. The baby gurgled.

"Wrong. I do need you."

Yeah, like he needed to stick his hand into an open fire.

She was stuck between telling a lie, which was a sin, and moving their relationship into a new realm, which would also be a sin. She didn't know what to do.

"I care about you, Chris. It's just that…"

His mouth formed a hard line. "What? My bank account's not big enough for a Harcourt?"

"No." She grabbed his shirt collar. "Don't think that. Don't ever think that. I'm worried about you, not me."

"Worried about me? Why? What are you talking about?"

Dismayed to have blurted out the worry, she tilted away and grew quiet. "I have a baby, Chris. You're a pastor."

His expression went rock hard. "So?"

She flushed red hot. "Don't be naive. It matters."

"Not to me. The way I look at it, everyone makes mistakes. Some are just more obvious than others." He glanced down at the baby on his knees. "And to tell the truth, it's kind of hard to look at this little guy and even think the word *mistake*."

"I know," she said softly. Gabriel wasn't a mistake, but she had made plenty that Christopher didn't know about. "I just think we'd be better off as friends, that's all."

If only he knew how despicable she really was, he wouldn't even want that much.

"Don't you believe in second chances?"

Couldn't he see how damaging a relationship with her could be to his career as a minister? "I don't think so."

"What about the second chance Christ gave you?"

"That's different."

"Is it?" he asked.

She didn't know.

As his eyes narrowed in thought as though some grand scheme took shape inside his brilliant mind, Christopher said, "Give me the rest of the summer to prove you wrong."

When she hesitated, torn between what she wanted and what she knew was best, he laughed and tapped her on the chin. "A couple of months. That's all I'm asking. I might be worth it."

Oh, he was worth it all right. But was she?

The sun moved toward the western horizon and in the near distance on the square, the drum and fife corps warmed up for the evening march through town. Ashley slid the diaper bag onto the handle of Gabriel's stroller while Chris lowered the baby into the seat. Her son chattered and kicked as if he'd been waiting all day for Christopher's company.

She could totally understand the feeling. On the days she didn't see him, which were few, life felt flat and gray.

In civilian clothes, as they jokingly called jeans and T-shirts, they headed out of the old section of Williamsburg, past William and Mary College toward modern Williamsburg.

Ashley was playing with fire and she knew it, but like

some kind of warped personality, she couldn't seem to resist Chris's gentle courtship. He didn't push hard, but he did push. Showing up at odd moments to whisk her off for a stroll through the gardens or for a refreshing soda—or times like these when he came by after work with the offer to walk her and Gabriel to the town park.

Dating was difficult with a baby tagging along and she figured that was a good thing. She didn't date. Couldn't date. But Chris never let Gabriel's presence bother him. In fact, he seemed to enjoy her son. And to tell the truth, her heart melted at the sight of this big, strong but gentle man giving her son the masculine attention he craved.

Gabriel needed a father. A father like Chris.

She shook her head to dispel the thought. Chris had asked for the summer and she'd give him that. She'd give herself that. But from there, they had no future. Here in Williamsburg for the summer only, he and his career as minister were safe from her sins. Outside this town, her mistakes were waiting like hungry wolves to hurt everyone.

Chapter Four

Ashley stood back to admire the glorious handcrafted dress she'd designed for the contest. Made of watered silk, only the wealthiest planter's wife could have worn this in the eighteenth century. This was her masterpiece, and after weeks of painstaking work both in the shop and at home, the rich burgundy gown was completed.

"It's perfect, Ashley," Milly said from her spot at the design table. "You've done an excellent job."

Ashley fussed with the lace sleeves. "Do you think it has a chance to win?"

"As good a chance as any other." Milly pushed her wire rims higher on her nose. "Are you wearing it to the Garden Party after the judging?"

Ashley nodded. Each year on July Fourth, a garden party was held at the Governor's Palace. Employees and interns were requested to attend in full colonial dress to create the perfect atmosphere for the tourists.

"I designed a cute little suit for Gabriel, too."

"What about your young blacksmith?"

"Milly, you are hopeless." And so was she. Sometimes she wondered why God brought Chris back into her life now, when she'd destroyed any hope of them being together for more than the summer. "Christopher is not my anything."

"Well, he wants to be, so wake up. He's a catch."

With a roll of her eyes, Ashley draped the carefully folded gown over the shade of Gabriel's buggy and started out the door. As much as she'd like to talk to someone about Chris, about the terrible confusion inside her, Milly was not the person. Since Gabriel's birth, she and her sister had been close enough to talk. Though Samantha was on a modeling assignment in South Africa, maybe she'd give her a call tonight anyway. She needed some advice badly.

"Talk to you later, Milly. I have to get this dress up to the ballroom before five."

She pushed out into the muggy July afternoon with Gabriel fast asleep. Though the sun shone brightly, thunder rumbled in the distance like an empty train. Hesitating, Ashley cast a cautious eye to the clouds. Water would ruin the gown, but unless her entry arrived on time, she hadn't a chance of winning. One disadvantage of Colonial living was the lack of modern conveyance at times like this.

After a minute of indecision, she pressed on, hurrying down the street. Most evenings this week thunder had rumbled but they'd had no rain. Today would likely be the same.

Three blocks into the walk, she was calling herself an idiot. The wind picked up and the sky darkened.

A block later, fat drops of rain splatted the top of her head. Frustration and dismay mounted with each hurried step.

After making certain Gabriel was covered, she flipped open her umbrella, held it close to the gown and pushed the buggy faster. Like always, she'd made the wrong decision and now she'd suffer the consequence.

She glanced behind her, considered turning back. She'd already passed all the open businesses but the palace was still some distance. Wheeling around, she headed toward an eatery one block away and directly into the now driving rain. Everyone with any sense had already ducked inside the shops and open buildings. Leave it to her to be caught out in a cloudburst.

Holding the umbrella like a shield, she pushed forward, blinded to all but the next step. By now, Gabriel was awake and howling. Water sluiced off the edge of the umbrella into her face, onto the buggy and the voluminous silk skirt.

Tears prickled the back of her eyelids. Sometimes she hated herself. She could do the stupidest things. Even God must think she was stupid today.

"Ashley!" Out of nowhere, Christopher appeared in front of her and in the next moment a canvas tarp blocked the rain.

"Chris, what are you doing out in this?"

"Rescuing the damsel in distress, I hope." He guided them, tarp aloft like a giant kite, down the street and into the restaurant. "I've always wanted to add that to my resume. Minister, blacksmith, knight in shining armor. Kind of has a ring to it, huh?"

Normally, his joke would have made her laugh and she would have replied in kind. Not this time. She was too busy hating herself.

Once inside the old building, Ashley bent to soothe the startled baby and examine the burgundy gown. All the while, she fought tears. "I should have known better than to chance it. I'm so stupid sometimes."

Reaching around her to take Gabriel, Chris frowned. "Why do you do that?"

"What? Tell the truth? That I'm a total mess-up?"

"Everyone messes up occasionally, Ashley. Cut yourself some slack. No one expected a cloudburst. I sure didn't." He hitched his chin toward a table. "Come on. Let's sit until this blows over."

She left the elegant dress draped inside Gabriel's carriage. "This is probably ruined now anyway."

"Maybe not. But if it is, would that be the end of the world?" He settled into a chair with Gabriel on his lap. The baby snuggled into Chris's chest and closed his eyes.

"No, I suppose not, but I wanted to win that contest." Still, Chris was right. It wasn't the end of the world. A spark of the ridiculous struck her as she cast a baleful glance toward the water-sprinkled dress. "I learned one thing from this. Watered silk does not really need watering."

"That's my girl. Turn that frown upside down." The corners of Chris's eyes crinkled at the childish rhyme. "Do you have anything else to enter?"

She shrugged. "Nothing that has a chance. I designed a fancy outfit for Gabriel, waistcoat and britches, everything, but it's not as elaborate as the gown."

"It's worth a shot, isn't it?"

She had little hope for winning now, but the contest was still an opportunity to get her work in front of interested people.

"Well, maybe." Her spirits lifted the slightest bit. Leave it to Chris to encourage her this way. No wonder she'd fallen in love with him.

Her heart stuttered and stopped, then started again. She loved a man of God, a man who needed a perfect wife, a wife with a clean slate. She wondered if God was angry at her for even considering such a thing.

"There you go, then," Chris was saying. "When the rain passes, if the gown is too damaged, we'll get Gabriel's duds and head on over to the palace." He glanced out the window at the brightening sky. "I stopped by your shop to ask you about the Garden Party this Saturday. Maybe we could go together."

Ashley didn't hesitate. She'd promised him the summer. And even though there was no hope for them beyond this, she wanted to be with him now.

"Don't we both have to attend anyway?" she said, teasing her way past the band of worry determined to strangle the joy of loving.

One masculine hand slapped the spot above his heart. "Ouch. There went my ego. A few minutes ago I was your white knight."

He still was. Always would be. "Do you still want us to come to church with you on Sunday?"

"Yes, and no backing out now. I've already told my friends that I'm bringing someone very special."

She had yet to hear him preach, though he'd asked her to come several times. This Sunday, a special Independence Day celebration was planned with fellowship afterward. The idea of meeting his congregation gave her the jitters but she'd promised. She breathed a secret prayer that no one in the congregation would recognize her name.

Within the walled confines of the Governor's Palace, music from a stringed quartet lilted over the lush, green maze of boxwood and the vibrant flower gardens. Interpreters in fancy dress milled about, chatting eighteenth century business with one another and the guests who had paid handily for the honor of attending the formal party.

Ashley wore the silk gown, and to Chris she was the most beautiful woman in the gardens. He knew she was disappointed about the contest and so was he. If she'd won, he could guarantee keeping her in Williamsburg for longer than a summer. Now there was only one way to keep her here. She cared for him. He was sure of it, but each time he tried to move their relationship closer to commitment, she backed away. Something bothered her.

He wished she'd trust him enough to confide in him. Somehow, someway, he'd break down the wall that separated them. He'd prayed all week about tonight and tomorrow, when she'd promised to attend church. He was certain once she met his friends and congregation, she would see how well she fit in, how much she could enjoy the life here, and how much he needed her at his side. Tonight and always.

He took two glasses of foamy punch and moved through the murmuring crowd to her side.

"Beautiful lady," he said, offering a glass.

"Flatterer." But she beamed at the compliment. "You're looking very handsome yourself."

He stroked four fingers over his embroidered weskit. "I happen to know the town's best seamstress. She makes me look good."

"Really? And who might this talented lady be?"

He leaned closer, loving the golden flecks in her brown eyes. "If you and your handsome son would care to accompany me around the lawns, I might be persuaded to tell you."

They both chuckled softly at the silliness and began to stroll the narrow pathways through the enormous gardens. When he reached for Ashley's hand, she slid hers easily into his. Such a simple act and yet he loved holding her hand, touching her soft skin, being with her. He wondered if she had any idea how much her quiet laugh and gentle insights meant to him. When he shared his dreams, she encouraged and admired. When he shared his worries, she listened.

Yes, he loved Ashley Harcourt, a girl some would call out of his league, but he knew God was the great equalizer. Their shared faith was enough.

The palace gardens encompassed several acres and

before he realized it, they were deep inside the elaborate holly maze.

"A person could get lost in here."

"Would that be so bad?" he asked.

Her smile was his answer, so they settled on a bench in a verdant nook and talked as night fell around them.

Lanterns were struck and the flicker of gas lights lit the evening with a romantic glow. And they talked on.

Chris felt a contentment tonight that had been missing in his life. Ashley and Gabriel gave him new purpose.

"We can watch the fireworks from here," Ashley said, "if Gabriel cooperates." Though he'd been awake most of the evening, the baby now slept, his long eyelashes shadowed on chubby cheeks.

"Sounds good to me." The fireworks were on the palace green in front of the palace. "As far as I'm concerned we can stay here forever."

"Why, Mr. Sullivan. You would compromise my honor by keeping me out here alone forever?"

Though Ashley joked, Chris didn't. "No, ma'am. I'd never do anything to compromise you in any way." He turned to face her, pulling her hands into his. "I was going to wait until summer's end to do this, but I've been waiting for you for years. I love you, Ashley."

She touched his cheek. "I know."

He held his breath, waiting. Would she finally admit what he knew was true? That she loved him, too?

Her answer came in a rustle of silk as she slid her arms around his neck and moved closer. Her soft breath mingled with his until he thought he'd die of waiting.

"I love you, too, Chris, but—"

He cut her off with a kiss. Tonight he wanted no buts, only the joyous knowledge that she loved him.

Chapter Five

Ashley awakened with a sense of hope so powerful she slid to her knees beside the bed and said a prayer of thanks.

Last night, she'd told Chris all that was in her heart. For once, she couldn't avoid the truth and hadn't wanted to. He deserved to know how loveable and wonderful he was. So she'd told him. She'd told him how happy he made her and how he filled her heart with plans and hopes and dreams. She'd admitted how she admired and respected him and how much she'd grown in her faith just from spending time with him.

And she'd pledged her love.

Part of her wanted to laugh and sing and shout from the courthouse balcony the great good news. The sensible part of her was scared silly. They were in love, and for now, that was enough. But would marriage be down the road? Could she take that chance? Chris kept telling her everything would work out, and he was so smart. Maybe he was right. Maybe she could move past her mistakes. Maybe God had forgiven her enough.

Now, sitting in his church, she watched her love in the pulpit, saw his eyes twinkle when he looked her way, and felt more special than she ever had in her life. Pastor Christopher Sullivan loved her.

When the service ended, he made his way through the small congregation to her side. Friendly faces gathered round to meet her. Though Christopher introduced her only as "my friend, Ashley," the parishioners smiled knowingly. Anyone watching them could see they were in love. Didn't it shine from her eyes like noonday sun?

Chris hoisted Gabriel onto one shoulder and placed his hand at her elbow, guiding her down a short hall to the fellowship room. A handful of church members ambled alongside chit-chatting. Some discussed the sermon, others asked about Gabriel, and still others discussed yesterday's Independence Day celebrations. They smiled and talked to her, not one of them suspicious or cold in any way.

Ashley breathed a prayer of thanks for the warm welcome. Maybe the dream was possible after all.

Ladies of the church bustled about setting out covered dishes and preparing the tables. Their good humored chatter blended with the clatter of pans and spoons and scraping chairs. Two teenage girls begged to play with Gabriel and carried him away like a special toy.

With Christopher deep in conversation with one of his elders, Ashley stepped into the kitchen section where the warm scent of fried chicken hovered in the air like ministering angels.

"This room smells fabulous," she said and then laughed along with the others, feeling better by the minute. "How can I help?"

A redhead with glasses looked up from the oven. "You could start filling cups with ice. Or slice the pies and cakes if you'd like."

Ashley dove in, happy to be useful and accepted. "There sure is a lot of food here."

A grandmotherly lady with rosy cheeks said, "Sure is, honey. Pastor Chris has a thing about feeding the needy. Well, we all do, but you know how he is."

The other ladies looked at her with smiling speculation.

"What Margie means," said the redhead, "is this. After our fellowship, the real work begins. We pack carry-out trays, load up the van and take dinner to all the shut-ins we know of, and the rest goes to the shelter down by the free clinic. Pastor does a lot of ministry work down there."

For half a minute, Ashley was transported back in time to the day of Gabriel's birth at the free clinic. A cold wave of anxiety washed over her. Would Chris expect her to go down there? Would she be recognized?

"Honey, you're the color of wallpaper paste. Are you okay?" Margie took Ashley's arm and guided her to a chair. A fashionable woman near her age, who'd said little, thrust a glass of iced tea into her hands.

With a self-conscious laugh, Ashley said, "I'm all right. It's just so warm in here."

"Hotter than the Fourth of July," Margie joked, swiping at her brow. With the bit of humor, Ashley's uncomfortable moment passed, but she couldn't shake the feeling that disaster waited like a crouching tiger.

When the meal was served, Ashley, nerves still jittery, sat at a long, plastic-covered table next to Chris and picked at her potato salad. The fashionable young woman, whose name was Paige, sat across from them. It didn't take a rocket scientist to realize Paige was interested in the handsome young pastor. A twinge of jealousy caught Ashley by surprise and she doubled her efforts to talk to the woman.

"Have you attended Crosspoint long?" she asked.

"A while." Paige smiled, but she looked at Ashley with an odd expression. "Something about you seems so familiar. What did you say your last name is?"

Ashley swallowed a new attack of nerves. "Harcourt. I'm not from this area."

"Harcourt. Harcourt." Paige tapped a fingernail on the table edge and stared. "You aren't related to the man over in Chestnut Grove that used to run the adoption agency, are you?"

Ashley's jitters turned to knee-knocking anxiety. Area newspapers had been filled with the story for months. "He was my grandfather."

"We all read about that. Ashley and her folks had no idea what her grandfather was doing," Chris said over a fork of baked beans.

"No, we didn't. No one is sorrier than we are for all the problems he caused."

Her grandfather Barnaby Harcourt had falsified birth records and basically bought and sold babies through the years. She shuddered to think his blood flowed through her veins. Some would call her a chip off the old block.

"I remember reading about that one girl, Kelly something I think," Paige went on. "Fascinating story. She and her birth mother had been living in the same town all those years and neither of them knew it."

Ashley wanted to change the subject, but her mind had frozen in fear.

"And then the mayor's wife tried to kill her so no one would discover that the mayor himself had fathered the girl and paid Barnaby Harcourt to get rid of her." Paige gave a happy shiver. "It was better than a soap opera. You remember reading it don't you, Chris?" She cast baby blues at Chris whose expression had darkened. "And then if that wasn't enough, someone found an abandoned baby on the doorstep, and he turned out to belong to one of the Harcourts."

The moment the words flew out of her mouth, Paige pretended to be surprised. She laid a manicured hand over her mouth and stared at Ashley. "That wasn't *you*, was it?"

Ashley knew she'd been set up. Paige had known all along.

Shaking all over, she glanced at Chris. The shock on his face was all she needed to see. With as much grace as she could muster with her whole world crumbling, she said, "Excuse me. I need to change my son."

"Ashley?" Chris shoved back from the table. "Wait."

But she couldn't. Grabbing Gabriel without explanation, she hurried out of the building and hailed a taxi.

The worst had happened. Christopher now knew her darkest shame. Worse, she had embarrassed him in front of his congregation. Shame was a tidal wave, sweeping her back to that frightening time when she'd made the worst mistake of her life. No excuse was ever enough to justify the sin she'd committed the day she'd left Gabriel on the doorstep of Tiny Blessings Adoption Agency. How could she expect Christopher to understand? She didn't understand herself.

"Where to, Miss?" the cabbie asked.

Her summer of hope and love was over. She'd known all along she couldn't have Chris. She'd even known better than to attend his church. Still, for that shining moment last night, she'd almost believed things would work out the way Chris promised.

But life didn't work that way. Some things couldn't be forgiven.

Might as well face the end and be done with it. Christopher didn't need a woman like her in his life.

"Chestnut Grove," she replied, and gave her parents' address, and, gripping her baby tightly, let the tears come.

At dusk, Ashley sat in the shady garden patio alongside her parents' pool. After explaining what had transpired with Chris, she wanted to be alone. Mother had Gabriel inside while Ashley tried to pray but she was too depressed. Tomorrow was soon enough to make a decision about her internship.

The patio door slid open but she didn't turn around. "I'll take him now, Mother, if you're tired."

No answer. She twisted around in her chair and her heart dipped low.

She might have known he would come. Chris wasn't a man to leave loose ends.

"I don't want to talk."

"Too bad. I do." He scraped a chair over the cobblestones and parked it beside hers. "After you left, Paige told me the whole story. The one she read in the paper, anyway. I want to hear it from you."

Shame suffused her. "Why?"

"Because I want to hear your side, what really happened."

The scent of hamburgers wafted on the wind. Someone in the neighborhood must be grilling. "I abandoned my baby. Period."

"There's more to it than that. I know how much you love him."

"That's why. Because I loved him. Because I was confused and stupid and sick."

"What kind of sick?"

"Mentally. Physically. Every way." She picked at her fingernail ashamed to look at the man she loved, now that he knew what kind of person she really was. "Mother and Dad were out of the country because of the adoption scandals. They didn't even know I was pregnant. We never talked anyway. I didn't think they'd care or help." Her voice fell to a whisper. "I was so scared, so very scared. And when the fever started…"

She shivered at the memory of the terrible sickness, a sickness so powerful she hadn't been able to remember where Gabriel was, couldn't remember if she'd fed him.

Chris's hand covered hers. Even in the heat of July her skin was cold.

"I sneaked out of the clinic with Gabriel an hour after his birth to come home. I wanted to think things through, figure out what to do. But then I got so sick. I couldn't take care of him. I couldn't stop shaking. And the fever was so bad, I thought I might die. And if I died, so would he. All I could think of was getting Gabriel to some place safe."

"So you took him to the agency."

She nodded. "Stupid, I know. So stupid."

"No. The natural instinct of a loving mother to protect her baby."

"Don't make excuses for me, Chris. I abandoned my son."

"And you can't forgive yourself."

"Could you?"

Instead of a pat answer, Chris took his time and thought about it. She appreciated that. Platitudes wouldn't cut it today. "I don't know, Ash. But I do know this. God forgave you when you asked Him into your life."

"But He remembers. I have to pay for what I've done."

"If you think that, you're aren't reading the same Bible I do. Jesus paid for your sins and your mistakes,

Ashley. All of them, even the ones you have trouble letting go of. Your past is washed away in a sea of God's forgetfulness, as far as the east is from the west. God doesn't hold your sin against you unless you keep on doing it."

The smallest flame of hope flickered. "Is that true? Or are you trying to make me feel better?"

"Both. I knew you were struggling with something heavy. I just wish you would have told me a long time ago."

"I'm sorry you had to find out this way, in front of everyone. I was so ashamed. Still am."

In trying to protect him, she'd only hurt him more. Since giving birth she understood love in a new light. Love was giving. Love never did harm. By not telling him everything, she'd set Chris up for harm.

"Now you know why I can't be with you. A fallen woman, a woman who would abandon her own child would be a detriment to a pastor. Just like today, no congregation would accept that. I'd ruin your career."

She couldn't do that to him. Not if she really loved him.

"You're wrong about that."

She shook her head, loose locks tumbling from the knot she'd twisted atop her head. "I don't think so."

"What if I left the ministry?"

"Absolutely not! You're a wonderful pastor. The people love you."

"After you left, I offered to resign."

Horror filled her. This was worse than she'd thought. "Oh, no, Chris. Oh, please say you didn't."

"The church wouldn't let me. But we had a long, fruitful discussion. That's why it took me awhile to get here. For some time now, the church has been helping me pray for a wife. I told them I'd found her. But like every one of us, she isn't perfect." He tapped her on the nose and smiled. "But close enough to perfect for me. And if they didn't have it in their hearts to follow the teachings of Jesus in such matters, then I couldn't be their pastor."

"I can't believe you did that."

"Believe it. Being a Christian means behaving like Christ. He taught love and compassion, not judgment and condemnation. Paige is a new Christian, too. She made a mistake today. She knows that now, and I hope you'll forgive her."

Forgive her? Ashley wanted to strangle her. Immediately, she squelched the thought. If she expected to be forgiven, she had to forgive. "Paige likes you."

"I know. But I'm in love with you. God put us together, Ashley. Don't tear us apart again."

God put them together. She liked the sound of that.

Like chocolate in July, her resistance melted. "Oh Christopher, I love you. I'm sorry for—"

He placed his fingertips over her lips. "Shh. No more apologies. All is forgiven."

Forgiven. The sweetest word ever spoken. At last, she understood the depth of God's love and forgiveness. Understood and accepted.

And as her true love pulled her into his arms for the

sweetest kiss, Ashley was finally able to leave the past behind and embrace the future, as a woman, as a mother and someday soon as a pastor's wife.

* * * * *

Though Ashley and Christopher have found their happily-ever-after, will things remain as rosy for the Tiny Blessings Adoption Agency?

Look for FOR HER SON'S LOVE by Kathryn Springer. The first book in "A Tiny Blessings Tale" miniseries.
In stores July 2007.

Love Inspired®

Celebrate Love Inspired's 10th anniversary with top authors and great stories all year long!

A Tiny Blessings Tale

Loving families and needy children continue to come together to fulfill God's greatest plans!

Look for these six new *Tiny Blessings* stories!

FOR HER SON'S LOVE BY KATHRYN SPRINGER
July 2007

MISSIONARY DADDY BY LINDA GOODNIGHT
August 2007

A MOMMY IN MIND BY ARLENE JAMES
September 2007

LITTLE MISS MATCHMAKER BY DANA CORBIT
October 2007

GIVING THANKS FOR BABY BY TERRI REED
November 2007

A HOLIDAY TO REMEMBER
BY JILLIAN HART
December 2007

Steeple
Hill®

Available wherever you buy books.

DELIVERS HEARTWARMING, INSPIRATIONAL ROMANCES.

On sale July 2007

Available wherever
books are sold,
including most bookstores,
supermarkets, drugstores
and discount stores.

Receive $1.⁰⁰ off

the purchase of any book from Love Inspired®.

Coupon expires December 31, 2007. Redeemable at participating
retail outlets in the U.S. only. Limit one coupon per customer.

RETAILER: Harlequin Enterprises Ltd. will pay the face value of this coupon plus
8 cents if submitted by the customer for this specified product only. Any other
use constitutes fraud. Coupon is nonassignable. Void if taxed, prohibited or
restricted by law. Void if copied. Consumer must pay any government taxes. Mail
to Harlequin Enterprises Ltd., P.O. Box 880478, El Paso, TX 88588-0478, U.S.A.
Cash value 1/100 cents. Limit one coupon per customer. Valid in the U.S. only.

11417-5

5 65373 00076 2   (8100) 0 11417

LITCICOUP

"Was he hurt?" Grey asked in a worried voice.

A Soldier's Heart

Marta Perry

Steeple
Hill®

Published by Steeple Hill Books™

Chapter One

She was keeping an appointment with a new client, not revisiting a high school crush. Mary Kate Donnelly opened her car door, grabbed the bag that held the physical therapy assessment forms and tried to still the butterflies that seemed to be doing the polka in her midsection.

What were the odds that her first client for the Suffolk Physical Therapy Clinic would be Luke Marino, newly released from the army hospital where he'd been treated since his injury in Iraq? And would the fact of their short-lived romance in the misty past make this easier or harder? She didn't know.

She smoothed down her navy pants and straightened the white polo shirt that bore the SPTC letters on the pocket. As warm as this spring had been, she hadn't worn the matching navy cardigan. The outfit looked new because it *was* new—just as new as she was.

Nonsense, she lectured herself as she walked toward the front stoop of the Craftsman-style bungalow. She was a fully qualified physical therapist and just because she'd chosen to concentrate on marriage and children instead of a career didn't make her less ready to help patients.

The truth was, her dwindling bank balance didn't allow her any second thoughts. She had two children to support. She couldn't let them down.

The grief that was never far from her brushed her mind. Neither she nor Kenny had imagined a situation in which she'd be raising Shawna and Michael by herself. Life was far more unpredictable than she'd ever pictured.

For Luke, too. He probably hadn't expected to return to his mother's house with his legs shattered from a shell and nerve damage so severe it was questionable whether he'd walk normally again.

Ruth Marino's magnolia tree flourished in the corner of the yard, perfuming the air, even though Ruth herself had been gone for nearly a year. Luke had flown from Iraq for the funeral. Mary Kate had seen him standing tall and severe in his dress uniform at the church. They hadn't talked—just a quick murmur of sympathy, the touch of a handshake—that was all.

Now Luke was back, living in the house alone. She pressed the button beside the red front door. Ruth had always planted pots of flowers on either side of the door, pansies in early spring, geraniums once the danger of frost was past. The pots stood empty and forlorn now.

There was no sound from inside. She pressed the button again, hearing the bell chime echoing. Still nothing.

A faint uneasiness touched her. It was hardly likely that Luke would have gone out. Rumor had it he hadn't left the house since he'd arrived, fresh from the army hospital. That was one reason she was here.

"You went to high school with him." Carl Dickson, the P.T. center's director, had frowned at the file in front of him before giving Mary Kate a doubtful look. "Maybe you can get him in here for an assessment. He's refused every therapist we've sent. You certainly can't do any worse."

She had read between the lines on that. She was new and part-time, so her hours were less valuable. Dickson didn't want to waste staff on a patient who wouldn't cooperate, but he also didn't want to lose the contract from the U.S. Army if he could help it.

She pressed the bell again and then rapped on the door, her uneasiness deepening to apprehension. What if Luke had fallen? His determination to reject every professional approach, even simple acts of kindness, left him vulnerable.

The knob refused to turn under her hand. Kicking the door wouldn't get her inside, tempting as it was, and if Luke lay helpless, he couldn't answer.

She stepped from the stoop and hurried around the side of the house toward the back door. She'd grown up less than two blocks away, in the house where her parents still lived. Luke had been at their place constantly in those days, shooting hoops on the improvised driveway court. A frayed basketball hoop still hung from the Marino garage, mute testimony to Luke's passion for sports.

The back porch had the usual accumulation—a forgotten rake, a trash can, a couple of lawn chairs leaning against the wall. She hurried to the door and peered through the glass at the kitchen.

At first she thought the figure in the wheelchair was asleep, but Luke roused at her movement, fastening a dark glare on her. He spun the wheels of the chair, but she didn't think he was planning to welcome her in. She opened the door and stepped inside, closing it behind her.

"Don't you wait to be invited?" The words came out in a rough baritone snarl. Luke spun the chair away from her, as if he didn't want to look at her.

Or, more likely, he didn't want her to look at him.

Her throat muscles convulsed, and she knew she couldn't speak in a normal way until she'd gotten control of herself. But Luke—

The Luke she remembered, as a high school football hero, as a police officer, as a soldier when his reserve unit was called up, had been all strength and muscle, with the athletic grace and speed of a cheetah and a relaxed, easy smile. Not this pale, unshaven creature with so much anger radiating from him that it was almost palpable.

She set her bag carefully on the Formica-and-chrome table, buying a few more seconds. She glanced around the kitchen. White-painted cabinets, linoleum on the floor, Cape Cod curtains on the windows—Ruth hadn't changed anything in years.

"I didn't think I had to stand on ceremony with an old friend," she managed to say, her voice gaining strength as she spoke. "Besides, I thought you might not let me in if I waited for an invitation."

He didn't answer the smile she attempted, sparing her only a quick glance before averting his face. "I don't want company, Mary Kate. You must have heard by now that I've made enemies of half the old ladies at church by rejecting their casseroles."

"Mom wouldn't appreciate being called an old lady, so you'd better not repeat that in her hearing."

Her mother had tried, and failed, in her quest to see that Luke had a home-cooked meal delivered by the church every night. Luke had apparently slammed the door in the face of the first volunteer and then refused to answer the bell for anyone else. After a week of refusals, her volunteers had given up.

"I didn't mean—" he began, and then stopped, but for just an instant she'd seen a glimmer of the old Luke before his face tightened. "I don't want visitors."

"Fine." She had to make her voice brisk, or else the pain and pity she felt might come through. She knew instinctively that would only make things worse. "I'm not a visitor. I'm your physical therapist."

He stared for a moment at the crest on her shirt pocket, swiveling the chair toward her. His legs, in navy sweatpants, were lax against the support of the chair.

"Doesn't your clinic have rules against you barging in without an invitation?" Once again the old Luke peeked through in a glimpse of humor.

"Probably." Definitely, and as the newest member of the staff, she couldn't afford to break any of the rules. On the other hand, she couldn't go back and admit failure, either. "Are you going to report me, Luke?"

His dark brows drew down like a slash over deep brown eyes. He'd once been the guy most often talked about in the girls' locker room, mostly because of those eyes. Smoky eyes, with a hint of mystery in them. Combined with the chiseled chin, firm mouth, jet-black hair and the glow of his olive skin, his looks and that faintly dangerous charm had had the girls drooling over him.

And he'd picked her. For a brief time, she'd gone out with the most sought-after guy in school. She hadn't thought of that in years, until today. Seeing him now brought it all flooding back—those days when you were up in the clouds one minute because that special guy had smiled at you and down in the depths the next because he'd smiled at someone else, too.

It hadn't lasted, of course. Maybe, in her naive first love, she'd been too clingy. Luke had made excuses, failed to return phone calls and finally had been seen in the back row of the movie theater with Sally Clemens. She'd given him back his class ring, kept her chin up and done her crying in private.

Luke just stared at her. Maybe he was remembering that, too. Finally, he shook his head, the stubble of his beard dark against the pallor of his skin. "No, I won't turn you in. Just beat it, okay?"

"Sorry, I can't." She pulled out one of the chrome kitchen chairs and sat down, reaching for the forms in her bag. "You're two weeks past due to report to the clinic for your evaluation and therapy. Why?"

His jaw clenched. "I've spent the last three months being poked and prodded by army experts. If they couldn't get me out of this chair, I don't think your outfit can. Just go back to your boss and tell him I appreciate it, but I don't need any more therapy."

His words twisted her heart. What he'd gone through would be horrible for anyone, but for Luke, who'd spent his life relying on his strength and skill on the playing field, then in the military and on the police force—well, this helplessness had to be excruciating.

Showing the pity and compassion that welled up in her was exactly the wrong way to react. To offer him sympathy would be to rub salt into an already agonizing wound.

But she couldn't walk away. He needed her help, or someone's help, whether he wanted it or not.

And she needed to make a success of this. A little flicker of the panic that had visited her too often since Kenny's death touched her. She had to provide financially for her kids, and that meant she had to prove herself at the clinic.

She took a steadying breath. "Sorry, Luke. I'm afraid I can't do that."

"Why not?" He shot the words at her, swinging the

chair closer to her in one fierce movement. "I don't need your therapy and I don't want it. Why can't you just understand that and leave me alone?"

His anger was like a blow. She stiffened in response. She couldn't let him chase her off, the way he had everyone else.

"I can't. And you don't really have a choice, do you? If you continue refusing to cooperate, the army will slap you back into a military hospital. And I don't think they'll let you bully them."

Bullying? Was that really what he was doing? All Luke knew was that he had to get rid of Mary Kate the way he'd gotten rid of everyone else who'd come to the door since he'd returned home.

And of all the people he didn't want to meet while sitting in a wheelchair, Mary Kate Flanagan Donnelly had to be somewhere near the top of the list.

He lifted an eyebrow, trying to find the right attitude to chase her away. "Looks like sweet little Mary Kate learned how to play hardball."

Judging by the annoyed look in those big blue eyes, she didn't care for that comment, but which part of it she disliked, he wasn't sure.

"It's been a long time since anyone's called me *sweet* and *little,* Luke. Welcome to the twenty-first century."

"Sorry." Funny to be alone with her now. He'd hardly seen her during the years after high school. She'd gone away to college—he'd enlisted in the service. When he'd come back and taken the job with the Suffolk Police Force, she and Kenny were already married, starting a family and moving in completely different circles. And then his reserve unit had been called up and he was gone again, this time to Iraq.

Once, he and Kenny had played football together. He and Mary Kate had dated. Funny to remember that now. They'd all been a lot more innocent then.

"I heard about Kenny." He pushed the words out, a reminder that he wasn't the only person suffering. "I'm sorry."

She paled under those Flanagan freckles, her lips firming as if to hold something back. When she'd walked in the door, slim and quick as the girl she'd been, he'd thought she hadn't changed at all.

Now he saw the differences—in the fine lines around her intensely blue eyes, in the determination that tightened her soft mouth. The hair that had once fallen to her shoulders in bright red curls was shorter now, curling against her neck, and it had darkened to an almost mahogany color.

She gave a curt nod in response to the expression of sympathy, as if she'd heard it all too many times. Well, then, she ought to understand how he felt. No help, no pity. Just leave me alone.

"The kids must be getting pretty big by now. Are they doing all right?" He put the question reluctantly, knowing that old friendship demanded it, knowing, also, that the more he treated her as a friend, the harder it would be to get her to leave.

Her face softened at the mention of her children. "Shawna's eight and Michael is six. Yes, they're doing fine. Just fine."

Something, some faint shadow in her blue eyes, put the lie to that repeated assertion. Tough on kids, to lose their father at that age. At least Kenny hadn't had a choice about leaving, like his father had.

He studied her, drawn out of his own circle of pain for a moment. Mary Kate's hands gripped the pad of forms a bit too tightly, her knuckles white. She still wore a plain gold band on her left hand.

How are you doing, Mary Kate? Really? How it must have pained Kenny to leave her, especially to let her see him dwindling away from cancer. No doubt Kenny would have preferred to go out in a blaze of glory fighting a fire.

Just as he'd rather have been standing a few feet closer to that bomb—to have died quickly and cleanly instead of coming home mutilated.

He glanced from her hands to her face, seeing there the look he dreaded. "I don't want your pity." He ground out the words, because if he didn't he might scream them.

"I'm not pitying you for your injury. I'm just sorry you've come home such a jerk." She leaned toward him. "Come on, Luke, admit it. You're not going to get out of this. The U.S. Army won't release you until they know they've done their best for you. You're lucky they let you come home for the therapy, instead of keeping you in the hospital."

"*Luck* is not a word I associate with this." He slapped his useless legs, getting a stab of pain in return.

"Fine." Her voice was crisp, as if she'd moved into a professional mode where friendship had nothing to do with them. "We both know I'm right."

He'd like to deny it, but he couldn't. If the army wanted him to have this therapy, he'd have it if they had to drag him kicking and screaming. Not that he could do much kicking.

"Okay." He bit off the word. "When you're right, you're right." At least with Mary Kate, he was over the worst—that moment when she looked at him and saw the ruin he was.

Surprise and relief flooded her face. "That's great." She shuffled the forms, picking up a pen. "We'll send the van for you tomorrow—"

"No."

She blinked. "But you said—"

"I'll do the therapy, but I'm not going anywhere. You can come here." Conviction hardened in him. He wasn't going out where anyone might see him. "And don't bother telling me you don't do that. I know you do in-home therapy."

"That's true, but we have equipment at the center that you don't have here. There's a therapy pool, exercise bikes, weight machines—all the things you might need." She dangled them like a lollipop in front of a recalcitrant child.

"So we'll improvise. That's the deal, M.K. Only you, only here. How about it?"

If she reacted to the high school nickname, she didn't let it show. Obviously she'd toughened up over the years. Still, she had to be easier to deal with than those hard-nosed army docs who'd outranked him.

"I can't authorize something like that."

"Then go back to your boss and get him to authorize it. Deal?"

She must have seen this was the best she could hope for, because she shuffled the papers together and shoved them back in her bag. Her lips were pressed firmly together, as if to hold back further argument.

"I'll try. I can't speak for the director, but I'll tell him what you said."

"Good." Well, not good, but probably the best he was going to get. He watched her hurry to the door, as if afraid he'd change his mind.

He wouldn't. He'd drag himself through whatever torture she devised, because he couldn't get out of it, but in the end it would amount to the same thing. Whether he was in a wheelchair or staggering around like an old man with a walker—either way, his life was over.

Returning to her car, Mary Kate was worried over what to do about Luke. The depth of his bitterness continued to shock her. She knew as well as anyone the important role played by the patient's attitude in healing. Luke's anger and isolation would poison any chance of wholeness if someone didn't do something to change it.

And, it seemed, either through chance or perhaps through God's working, that she was the one who was in a position to change that.

Did You put me in this situation? You must have a reason, but I don't see it. Seems to me I'm that last person who can help him deal with loss. I'm still struggling with that myself.

* * * * *

Can Mary Kate teach the reluctant soldier the kind of strength that brought her through her own dark times, or will tragic memories forever keep Luke and her apart?

Look for A SOLDIER'S HEART by Marta Perry available in stores April 24, 2007. Find it wherever books are sold, including most bookstores, supermarkets, drugstores and discount stores.

DELIVERS HEARTWARMING, INSPIRATIONAL ROMANCES.

On sale May 2007

Available wherever books are sold, including most bookstores, supermarkets, drugstores and discount stores.

Receive $1·00 off

the purchase of A SOLDIER'S HEART or any other book from Love Inspired®.

Coupon expires December 31, 2007. Redeemable at participating retail outlets in the U.S. only. Limit one coupon per customer.

RETAILER: Harlequin Enterprises Ltd. will pay the face value of this coupon plus 8 cents if submitted by the customer for this specified product only. Any other use constitutes fraud. Coupon is nonassignable. Void if taxed, prohibited or restricted by law. Void if copied. Consumer must pay any government taxes. Mail to Harlequin Enterprises Ltd., P.O. Box 880478, El Paso, TX 88588-0478, U.S.A. Cash value 1/100 cents. Limit one coupon per customer. Valid in the U.S. only.

11417-5

5 65373 00076 2   (8100) 0 11417

LITCICOUP2

DANGEROUS GAME
Lyn Cote

Steeple
Hill®

Published by Steeple Hill Books™

belonged. The murderer.

The morning of Grey Lawson's first day back in Winfield, she put her plan in motion. She hadn't gotten much sleep the night before. But now determined, she drove off Bear Paw Road onto the old logging road.

Glancing around, she was elated that there was no one on the road to see her turn off the main road near the hunting shack. She had to be careful and not give anyone a hint at what she planned to do.

Suspicion must fall on Grey Lawson. He shouldn't have come back here. She jounced over the ruts left from many summer rains and pulled close to the old log shack, facing the road. Her throat swelled with emotions— sorrow, regret, anger—the ones she usually kept at bay.

It was all Grey Lawson's fault that she was feeling this way. He'd come back to town as if he had a right to. It wasn't fair. But she'd hit on a way to make him pay, make them send him back to prison where he belonged. The murderer.

* * *

She sat behind the wheel of the old gray sedan. Her
nerves quivered with anticipation and fear. "I can do this.
I can," she repeated to herself over and over. But her
hands on the steering wheel trembled as if she had
Parkinson's just like Elsie Ryerson. I can't think about
that now. I have to do this for Jake.

Fog rolled, swirled around the gray sedan, making
the car almost invisible. She had chosen this location for
its relevance to Grey and his unforgivable crime against
Jake. Right off Bear Paw Road where it had all
happened over seven years ago. No one would mistake
the significance of this place. Now she waited to do what
she must do.

She heard a vehicle approaching, but couldn't see it
due to the mist. Do it now, she ordered herself. She
eased out of Park into Drive and pulled into the center
of the road. Trying to time it just right, she started
forward straight down the center line, picking up speed.
Right toward the oncoming vehicle.

Trish and Sheriff Harding drove up the gravel drive
through the heavy fog. They parked and then walked
from their vehicles through the cool moist air to Elsie
Ryerson's darkened house. A strange tightness wound
itself around Trish's lungs. She didn't want to be here
to question Grey Lawson. She could tell Keir didn't,
either. But an event had happened and this was their job.
We don't have a choice.

The sheriff knocked on the old plank door, and then
waited. It was well after midnight. Elsie and Grey were

probably sound asleep. But only a few minutes passed until the door opened a crack. "Who is it?" Grey asked.

Her tension constricting more, Trish waited for the sheriff to respond. *I don't want to do this.*

"Grey, it's Sheriff Harding and Deputy Franklin. We need to talk to you."

The door opened. Grey stood just inside the low-lit shadowy kitchen in gray sweats. "Come in," Grey said in a subdued voice.

Trish realized that he, too, must not want their visit to disturb his sleeping aunt. Trish and the Sheriff moved almost stealthily into the neat kitchen, closing the door gently against the damp night. Grey motioned them toward ladder-back chairs around the table. With a nod, the sheriff and then Trish eased into them. A faint trace of cinnamon hung in the air.

Grey sat down, facing both of them and murmured, "What's this about?"

Trish studied the shadows cast over his austere features by the only light coming from above the stove behind him. The essence of Grey Lawson beckoned her closer. She shifted on the hard seat.

"Where were you this evening?" the sheriff asked.

"Here." Grey eyed them with a visible wariness, but didn't ask them for more information.

Her face frozen into a noncommittal expression, Trish waited for the sheriff to proceed.

"You weren't out in your aunt's car tonight?"

"No." Grey's dark-lashed eyes sought hers.

She avoided his gaze, fought the urge to reach out and

reassure this grave man. The stove clock ticked over another minute.

"Can anyone corroborate your alibi?" the sheriff continued.

"What's this about?" Grey repeated.

"Just answer the question please."

An invisible but very effective veil came down over Grey's expression and his face turned to granite before her eyes. "My aunt was with me all day and all evening." Grey's words rasped her taut nerves.

The sheriff nodded. "That's what I thought, but I had to ask."

Grey did not repeat his question a third time. Just sat immobile and silent. Waiting.

Sheriff Harding gave her the barest of nods.

"There was an accident tonight or rather—" she had to stop to clear her throat "—a near miss on Bear Paw Road."

At her mention of the road where his life had altered direction forever, Grey didn't change expression by even a flicker of an eyelash. But a frost iced through her. Lives had ended that night.

"One of our summer residents was on his way home from a restaurant," she continued, each word costing her effort as she tried to sound matter-of-factly professional. "The mist had already impeded visibility. A late-model sedan, either gray, silver-blue or green drove toward him right down the center line. This took place at almost the same spot where…where your accident took place."

"Was he hurt?" Grey asked in a strained voice.

"No," the sheriff replied. "But your aunt can vouch for your whereabouts all of tonight?"

Trish exhaled deeply, trying to release the strain from this interrogation. She watched Grey process the muted accusation. He stiffened, drawing himself up straighter. His jaw hardened.

"So you think that I'd leave my aunt alone," Grey said with sharp sarcasm. "Take her car and drive back to the site of my accident and try to kill another innocent driver?"

"No." Trish's denial came quickly. Blood rushed to her face. She curled her fingers into her hands to keep them from reaching for Grey's sleeve. Why did she connect with him so much? Why did she want to touch this man?

"No," the sheriff agreed equably. "But you know that many people around here will unfortunately jump to just that conclusion. We came to question you so we can tell them you have an alibi."

Grey grimaced and looked toward the kitchen window, shrouded with gray mist. "Right," he muttered.

Trish knew that her father would revel in this latest occurrence. *What's going on here, Lord? This doesn't make any sense.*

"Is there something wrong?" Elsie's frail voice came from the hallway. She stepped into the kitchen in a worn flannel robe and slippers.

Grey hopped up.

Sheriff Harding rose, also. "Mrs. Ryerson, sorry we woke you."

"I sleep lighter and lighter all the time. What's wrong?"

Grey gently guided his aunt onto a kitchen chair.

The sheriff didn't sit back down. Reading this signal, Trish rose, too. "We were just checking with your nephew," the sheriff replied, "about his whereabouts this evening—"

"He's been with me almost constantly since he arrived home." Elsie glanced up at Grey who stood with a hand on her shoulder.

"That's what Grey told us," the sheriff said. "We just wanted to get his statement straight first, so unwarranted suspicion wouldn't fall on him."

Grey's presence filled the small room and Trish tried to keep her attention on the task at hand. But her eyes kept sliding sideways, catching glimpses of the handsome man so near, yet so removed. An invisible wall of history separated them.

Soon, she and the sheriff said their farewells and walked out into the misty night again. Grey's presence still summoned her to turn back, to offer to let him rest his head on her shoulder. She could feel the phantom touch of his hair upon her cheek.

Trish wrenched herself back to reality. How effective would their attempt at averting unfounded suspicion be? People would probably think that Elsie would say anything to keep her nephew from going back to prison.

But they would be mistaken. If Elsie Ryerson said Grey had been home with her at the time of the near miss, that's just where he'd been. Trish had zero doubt about that. So that left the question, who wanted to cast guilt on to Grey by playing such a stupid, dangerous game?

With a queasy feeling, Trish wondered where her father had been this evening.

The next morning, Sunday, dawned gray and windy, one of those harsh fall days that hint at the winter to come. With each step Grey took up to the church door, his confidence shriveled. Aunt Elsie must also be under a similar strain because earlier she'd even asked if he'd like to visit a different church today. Grey had been tempted by her offer. But why postpone the inevitable?

This had been his aunt's church since she was a child; he wasn't going to make her change churches just because Noah Franklin was an elder here. Over seven years ago, why hadn't it occurred to Grey that everything he did reflected for good or ill on his aunt? *How could I have been so selfish?*

He tried to focus on the fact that he was once again coming into the Lord's house, a place where he could worship the God of forgiveness, the God of second chances. The God who had become his refuge and strength in prison.

Obviously in high spirits, Elsie waved at friends as they made their way up the aisle to his aunt's favorite pew. Grey tried to focus on the church and not the people. But the back of Noah Franklin's head drew his gaze.

As always, Noah was sitting on the aisle in the left front pew. In the pew behind him sat most of Trish's family. Andy, whom he'd met again on his first day back sat beside his wife. Chaney, just a few years older than

Trish and then Mick, the youngest. Chaney glanced over his shoulder and froze when he saw Grey.

Grey looked down, avoiding Chaney's gaze as he led Elsie to her accustomed pew. Just as he reached it, he couldn't help himself. He looked again at the Franklin family ahead and noticed that a few of their widowed aunts also sat in the family pew. The women cast him dark glances; Trish an unreadable one.

Grey and his aunt sat down six rows behind them. He hoped none of the rest of the Franklins would look around again. The expression on Chaney's face had been far from welcoming. Grey sat low in his seat and wished he could blend unseen into the old oak pew.

The organ prelude ended and Grey noted that Sylvie Patterson, the local bookstore owner, still played the organ on Sundays. She must be nearing thirty just like Chaney and she had kindly sent him books periodically while he did time. The service began. Grey found it harder and harder to concentrate on the opening hymns. Even when Grey was looking at the hymnal, the back of Noah's head kept drawing his gaze.

The hymn ended and Noah Franklin walked to the pulpit to read this Sunday's scripture. The older man looked like an Old Testament prophet, dressed in a black suit, tie and white shirt. Without looking at the congregation, he took out drugstore reading glasses and began reading the parable of the Unforgiving Servant, from the Book of Matthew.

In the midst of the reading, Noah glanced up, gazing out at the faces before him. And then he abruptly stopped.

Silence. Everyone looked up from their pew Bibles. Their gazes followed Noah's and soon the whole church was staring at Grey. Caught in the older man's cross-hairs, Grey froze. The silence went on. Wind brushing the windows was the only sound.

"You," Noah finally pronounced the single word accusation. "You."

Sitting with her family, Trish felt as though she were standing beside a large gong someone had just struck. Her father's voice echoed and vibrated through her. Earlier, when she'd glanced back and glimpsed Elsie and Grey entering the sanctuary, she'd known that he would balk at Grey's presence. But not out loud. Not in front of the whole congregation. Not from the pulpit.

"Get out," her father ordered, his quivering hand pointing toward Grey. "Get out of this church."

The pastor, William Ray, looked stunned where he sat beside and just behind her father. Whispers flew around the sanctuary.

"Out!" Noah ordered.

Trish rose. She opened her mouth to object.

But Pastor Ray also rose. "Noah," he said sharply, "what are you doing?"

Noah stepped away from the pulpit and stormed down the steps and up the aisle.

Pastor Ray pursued Noah. Just as the older man reached Grey's pew, the pastor grabbed Noah's elbow and pulled him around. "What are you doing, Noah? You're disrupting the service."

Noah tried to shake the pastor's grip off, but couldn't. "Let me go. If this murderer won't leave, I'll make him."

Grey had risen.

Trish watched the color drain and then return to Grey's face, leaving it a blotchy red and white.

After another attempt at breaking the pastor's grip, Noah turned back to Grey. "Get out. I won't have you in my church."

Trish's breath caught in her throat. She couldn't decide whether she should join the threesome or hang back. Would she ease or worsen the situation? With her father, it was hard to predict.

"You do not own this church, Noah," Pastor Ray stated loud and clear. "You do not have the right to tell someone to leave."

"He killed my twin brother!" Noah shouted. "He has no right to sit in this church with decent people!"

Others rose in their pews. "Sit down, Noah. Please," someone said. Similar murmurs seconded this.

"Noah, anyone who comes into this church is a sinner and no sin is greater than any other," Pastor Ray stated. "Grey Lawson did not *murder* your brother. It was all a tragic drunk-driving accident and Grey has paid seven years in prison for his part in it." Pastor Ray looked up at Grey. "You are welcome in this church, Grey. I was happy to see you come today." He held out his other hand toward Grey.

Noah roared and finally wrenched himself free of Pastor Ray. "I won't have it! I pay your salary, Pastor!"

"Well, don't we all? Even Elsie?" Florence declared from the Franklin pew.

Others voiced support for this view. "You don't own this church, Noah Franklin."

Grey moved to leave. "I don't want to cause trouble—"

But Pastor Ray now wouldn't release Grey's hand. "You are welcome here and you will sit down." He looked at Noah. "And this service will continue. Noah, I believe you were reading today's scripture."

The three men stood in a tense tableau. Again, the sanctuary fell silent. Trish could hear her heart beating in her ears. Would her father listen to the pastor or escalate his vendetta?

At last, when Trish's tension had reached the point where she thought she couldn't stand it, her father charged down the aisle and out the church doors. They slammed behind him. Like a gust of December wind through pine boughs, sighs of shock and dismay rustled through the church.

Pastor Ray said, "Grey, your aunt told me that you had rededicated your life to Christ in prison. Is that true?"

Grey only nodded.

"Then let me extend to you the hand of fellowship." Pastor Ray clasped both Grey's hands in his.

"Thank you, Pastor."

Trish could hardly hear Grey's reply.

Pastor Ray urged Grey to sit back down. Then the pastor leaned over Grey to take Elsie's hand. "I know you've been waiting and praying for this day a long time, Elsie."

Elsie wiped her eyes with an old lace hankie and nodded.

The pastor then strode back up the aisle toward the pulpit. He paused by Trish. "I think it's time we had a woman read the scriptures occasionally. Trish, will you come up and finish the reading for your father?"

More whispering.

Nonplussed, Trish simply obeyed, following him up to the pulpit. Pastor Ray sat again in his chair and Trish tried to calm her cantering heart and lungs. She cleared her throat and lifted the Bible slightly. She began again.

Grey listened to Trish's voice gain confidence, becoming stronger, surer as she read the story of the servant who'd been forgiven much but who hadn't been forgiving with another servant. Her bright hair gleamed in the pale autumn light and against the oak-wood and white-plaster interior. Dressed in fall colors, she radiated a warmth, a cheer that brightened the room. Like a warm flame, she drew Grey toward her—an antidote to the chill left by her father.

From Noah Franklin, he'd expected shock and hostility. But never a public confrontation during the worship service. *Did I do right in coming here, Lord? I didn't mean to cause a rift in Your body, this church.*

After church, Grey tried at first to hurry his aunt out and home, but gave up. It seemed that everyone in the congregation wanted to talk to him or Elsie or both. Everyone had an opinion about his homecoming, Noah, and this morning's event. Grey stood as a silent sentinel beside Elsie.

Out of the corner of his eye, he noted many of the Franklins leave by the far aisle to avoid him. Again, Chaney, with a little boy obviously his son at his side, glared at Grey. But Penny and Andy, who still looked pale and moved slowly, came around the pew to thank him again for his help the night of the deer accident.

Where had Trish disappeared to? Grey finally was able to get Aunt Elsie out into the aisle and turned toward the door.

Out of nowhere, Trish appeared, offering her hand to him. "I'm glad to see you here this morning, Grey."

He couldn't doubt her sincerity. What made Trish Franklin tick? "I'm sorry," he mumbled, "about your dad. And everything." He made himself let go of her soft hand.

Trish inhaled deeply, but merely shrugged. She patted Elsie's arm and spoke softly to her. Then naturally as if he'd never been away and they'd been friends forever, she joined them in walking toward the doors.

Grey could hardly wait to escape. Trish should know better than to be seen walking with him.

Finally out in the furious north wind, Grey hurried his aunt to the Chrysler and helped her inside. Trish went to her red SUV and waved farewell to them. He made himself look away.

As he shut his aunt's door, he looked over the hood of the car and saw two of Trish's aunts still staring at him from down the street. Their sour unfriendly expressions chafed him like the violent wind. Florence's earlier retort aimed at Noah didn't mean she'd forgiven Grey. She just didn't like Noah much. And Noah had had five brothers, all dead now. All had been older than Noah except his twin brother, Jake. Jake Franklin—the man Grey had killed in a head-on collision seven years ago when he'd driven drunk one night, one of many drunken nights.

Sunday evening she slid behind the wheel of the hidden gray sedan.

She'd almost decided not to try another game of chicken. After her first near miss, her weak heart had pounded for almost an hour. Nausea had hit her in violent waves. Afterward, she'd been so relieved that her "victim" had been one of the summer residents, a stranger to her. She didn't want to scare anyone she knew out of their wits. Now she decided that this couldn't be helped. She had to risk another game of chicken. She had to.

Because this morning Grey Lawson had had the nerve to come to church before God and everybody. It wasn't right. Just recalling it, she boiled with resentment, sour bile filling her mouth. Noah had stood up to him. But a fat lot of good that had done her. The murderer had stayed in his seat and afterwards been greeted like a returning hero.

So grateful for the fog, she started the rough-sounding motor and drove down the rutted road, rocking on bad shocks. She positioned herself at the same point off Bear Paw Road and waited, listening for oncoming traffic. The tourist season had slowed from summer, but she hoped for another stranger to come unsuspecting into her trap.

In her mind, she went through the maneuvers she'd planned. Out of the mist, she'd drive straight at the oncoming vehicle. And at the last minute, she'd swerve to her right since she figured most drivers would swerve to their right, as well. And then she'd drive on up Bear Paw Road around the bend and disappear off toward her shed. Then she'd park the car—

She heard a motor ahead in the mist. She drove into position and began to gain speed. The other vehicle purred closer. Closer. Closer.

The other driver hit his brakes. His horn. She swerved to her right. He swerved to his left—not his right!

The oncoming car was dead ahead! She screamed and twisted the wheel.

Trish was driving slowly down Bear Paw south of her father's place.

Then she saw a car off on the shoulder. She hit her brakes and slowed, pulling up behind it. Leaping out, she ran to the driver's side and peered in. The driver was slumped over the steering wheel. She wrenched open the car door and felt for his carotid pulse. She found it and he was breathing. She realized then that this car was quite near the same spot as Grey's long-ago accident.

And very close to the recent near miss. What was going on here? A mere coincidence? She shook her head as if resisting this new worry. No time to stand around thinking. She lifted her cell phone from her belt and speed-dialed dispatch and reported the accident.

The near miss and now this accident, she felt as if matters were mounting, spiraling, spinning out of control.

The injured man moaned and shifted, evidently in pain. This brought her back to the problem at hand.

"Sir, you've been in an accident," she said. "Try not to move much. I don't know the extent of your injuries. I'm a deputy sheriff. I've called for help."

The middle-aged man lifted his head and blinked at her. "Some nut forced me off the road." He shook his head as if trying to clear it. "Someone in an old car. Barely missed him."

Great, just great. Had this been another game of chicken? If so, this time it had left a person injured. "Try to stay calm. Help's on the way." She patted his shoulder. Her ears strained to hear sirens. *Hurry up. Come on. Hurry.*

The Sunday night now past had been long, dismally damp and frustrating. At just before eight o'clock on Monday morning, Trish stood talking to Sheriff Keir Harding at the front of the town hall.

"I heard there was another game of chicken on Bear Paw last night," Florence LaVesque queried as she came upon them.

Dread for how this might affect Grey shivered its way through Trish. Who wanted to cause him more trouble? Who might be stacking the deck against Grey?

"A motorist was forced from the road last night," Sheriff Keir replied in a repelling tone. "He's at the Ashford hospital with minor injuries. Bear Paw Road has been blocked to all traffic around the scene of the accident. Two of my deputies have been on guard there all night and we'll begin gathering evidence as soon as daylight permits."

A few minutes later, Trish climbed into her red SUV. For a moment, she rested her weary head back against the headrest. A night without sleep and one family crisis after another had left her drained. Grey appeared at her window. She rolled it down. "Hi." She tried to smile, but her lips quivered. With effort, she kept her hand from reaching for his.

Grey handed her a thermos. "Elsie made coffee."

Trish fought to control her trembling lips, pulling together the trace of a smile. "Just...what I needed."

He pulled a plastic bag and a paper napkin from his jacket pocket. "And here's one of her cinnamon rolls. She knew you probably hadn't eaten anything since yesterday."

"I haven't but..."

"I'll drive," Grey said, opening the door and nudging her to move over, "while you eat and drink."

She knew she should object but she didn't have the strength. Besides, everything within her clamored to have Grey near. *I shouldn't feel this way, but I can't help myself.* She slid over and let him take the driver's seat. She twisted off the red cap from the vintage plaid thermos and poured steaming coffee into it. Then she opened the sandwich bag and let the fragrances of butter and cinnamon soothe her and whet her groggy appetite.

"You've had an awful week," Grey commented.

"Tell me about it," she muttered, concentrating on eating the roll. Or trying to focus on it.

"It will get better." He stated the words with unmistakable assurance. These words, plus the coffee and roll, revived her strength.

Those were the last words they exchanged for the duration of the drive. She watched his sure motions as he drove, studied his blunt, competent fingers, his long sinewy arms. Unlike the men in her family who turned out tall and broad like lumberjacks, Grey had the lean build of a runner. Their quiet ride settled her nerves and the hot coffee woke her finally and fully.

As Trish and Grey reached the scene of last night's game of chicken, the sheriff pulled up beside them. "Trish, you and I are going to relieve the deputies standing guard."

Trish didn't know how she should feel about this order. Technically, she was off duty today, but solving the mystery was important, too. A multitude of emotions vied for her attention. Instead she merely nodded and handed Grey the thermos.

"No, you keep it." He held up his hands. "I had breakfast before I came." Then he was off, walking toward home.

She climbed out of her SUV, and, without a word, the sheriff and Trish began their meticulous examination of the crime scene. He took one side of the road, she the other. She walked along the edge of the pavement, not wanting to disturb the soft gravelly shoulder, which might still harbor clues. She picked up a fallen branch and used it to stir the leaves. After no sleep all night, she heard herself breathing in the cottony quiet of the still misty dawn.

With the stick, Trish nudged aside more fallen leaves, looking for anything that had come from a human being or a car. Inexplicably, her mind drifted back to Grey driving her here. How did he manage to captivate her? Why couldn't she just ignore him?

Was it because, just like before, he'd brought her exactly what she'd needed? This time it had been sustenance and reassurance. The simple kindness of hot coffee, food, driving—taking care of her for a short while—had comforted her. Grey somehow projected a strength that had made her feel stronger.

"Trish!" Keir shouted. "Come here!"

Trish jogged over to the sheriff, who'd begun searching the opposite side of the road. When she got there, she saw that he was pointing to a hubcap that had come to rest against a tree trunk.

"See here." He pointed downward toward the fresh imprint of the hubcap's trail through the damp soil. "This could be from the perpetrator's car." The sheriff spoke with satisfaction.

Trish hoped that this was true. Something had to start going right. "It looks fresh and that track where it rolled is definitely fresh. This could be the break we need."

* * * * *

As Trish gets involved with Grey, she'll have to tread carefully, professionally and personally. And with a killer determined to frame him for crimes past and present, Grey can only pray that Trish won't suffer for his sins...

Don't miss Lyn Cote's DANGEROUS GAME, available in stores May 8, 2007 wherever books are sold.

Love Inspired. SUSPENSE

DELIVERS RIVETING, INSPIRATIONAL ROMANCES.

On sale May 2007

Available wherever
books are sold,
including most bookstores,
supermarkets, drugstores
and discount stores.